STEP
THIS
WAY
FOR
ANOTHER
GASKITTS
STORY

WELCOME

First U.S. edition 2002

Library of Congress Cataloging-in-Publication Data

Ahlberg, Allan.
The woman who won things / Allan Ahlberg ; illustrated by Katharine McEwen. —1st U.S. ed.
p.   cm.
Summary: As Mr. Gaskitt takes a series of jobs and Mrs. Gaskitt keeps winning prizes, their nine-year-old twins, Gus and Gloria, follow a substitute teacher who seems too good to be true.
ISBN 0-7636-1721-0
[1. Humorous stories.] I. McEwen, Katharine, ill. II. Title.
PZ7.A2688 Wn 2002
[fic]—dc21   2001035478

2 4 6 8 10 9 7 5 3 1

Printed in Italy

This book was typeset in Stempel Schneidler.
The illustrations were done in watercolor and crayon.

Candlewick Press
2067 Massachusetts Avenue
Cambridge, Massachusetts 02140

visit us at www.candlewick.com

MEOW!

Allan Ahlberg

The Woman Who Won Things

illustrated by

Katharine McEwen

CANDLEWICK PRESS
CAMBRIDGE, MASSACHUSETTS

Contents

Meet The Gaskitts

(and Horace's friend)

Mrs. Gaskitt

A taxi driver
and loving mother
who likes to
enter contests.

Mr. Gaskitt

A fond hard-working
father who always
takes any job
he can get.

Gus and Gloria Gaskitt

Nine-and-a-half-year-old twins.

Horace Gaskitt

A ginger-and-white cat
who likes to argue
with his friend.

No, I don't!
Yes, you do!
No, I don't!
Yes, you do!
No, I . . .
Yes, you . . .
No . . .
Yes . . .

Horace's Friend

A black cat
who likes to argue
with Horace.

The Gaskitts' Doormat

Mostly welcoming.

Sometimes grumpy.

Sometimes rude.

Chapter One
Mrs. Gaskitt's Luck Begins

One morning in the month of May

Mrs. Gaskitt got up.

Good morning, Mrs. Gaskitt!

She came downstairs, gave Horace a bowl

of Crunchy Mice,

and gave his

Thanks, Mrs. Gaskitt!

friend one too.

He was there

on a visit.

Mrs. Gaskitt got

Gus and Gloria up,

gave *them* their breakfasts,

and sent them off to school.

She read the paper,

drank a cup of tea,

picked up the mail

as it came tumbling

through the mailbox,

opened the door . . .

. . . and kissed the mailman!

9

But what about *Mr.* Gaskitt?

Never mind—

he *was* the mailman.

It was his latest job.

10

Meanwhile, Gus and Gloria were in the playground, watching—Oh no!—their poor teacher, Mrs. Fritter, falling off her bike at the school gates.

Mrs. Fritter hit the pavement
with a terrible bang,
got some nasty cuts and bruises
on her arms and legs, and had to go home.

Back in the kitchen,
Mrs. Gaskitt was opening the mail.
There was a gas bill
and a phone bill
and a postcard from
Grandma Gaskitt on vacation in Spain.

There was a vet's appointment for Horace . . .

and one more envelope.

Mrs. Gaskitt opened it.

Congratulations!

"Congratulations, Mrs. Gaskitt!"
said the letter.
"You have won first prize in our

most amazing contest."

"Wow!" cried Mrs. Gaskitt.

"This must be my lucky day."

Chapter Two
One Little Question

Half an hour later, a van stopped

outside the Gaskitts' house.

It had Mrs. Gaskitt's prize in it:

A YEAR'S SUPPLY

OF CRUNCHY MICE.

"All I did was answer

one little question," said Mrs. Gaskitt.

"Fancy that," said the van man.

"And make up one little caption."

"This must be your lucky day," the van man said.

Mrs. Gaskitt's prize filled the kitchen.

Horace's friend was amazed.

So was the doormat.

So was Horace.

"This must be

my lucky day,"

he thought.

WOW!

MICE

14

Back at the school, a substitute teacher
had arrived in Gus and Gloria's classroom.

This substitute teacher was rather short
and rather wide.
She had silvery hair,
dangly earrings,
a big smile . . .

"Hello, dearies!"

. . . and a huge suitcase.
On wheels.

"My name," she said, "is Mrs. Plum."
And she *opened* the case.

Meanwhile, back in the kitchen,

Horace and his friend were purring loudly and

gazing up at the piles

and piles of Crunchy Mice.

The word had spread.

Horace's other friends were

at the window, peeping in.

"I bet that would

last me . . . a year!"

cried Horace.

"Well, it would," said his friend.

"It's a year's supply."

"Oh, yeah," said Horace.

"Or half a year's supply

for two cats," said his friend.

"Yeah," said Horace.

"Or a month's supply

for twelve cats."

"Yeah!"

"Or a day's supply

for three hundred and sixty-five cats!"

"YEAH!"

"Or a *party*," meowed Horace's friends

from outside. "For us."

Chapter Three
Mrs. Plum's Suitcase

Mrs. Plum took out of her suitcase:

a ball of yarn and some knitting,

a photograph in a silver frame,

a vase of flowers (plastic),

a small guitar,

a sandwich maker,

a pair of pink fluffy slippers,

and a box of

chocolates.

There was silence in the room.
The children gazed in wonder
at Mrs. Plum,
the knitting,
the sandwich maker,
and the chocolates.
"This must be *our* lucky day,"
they thought.

Mrs. Plum put the flowers
and the photograph on her desk,
and the slippers on her feet.
She opened the box of chocolates
and popped one into her mouth.
"Now then, dearies, let's get started."

The day went by in Mrs. Plum's class
and the children loved it.
They had cooking lessons with
the sandwich maker,
science lessons *fixing*
the sandwich maker, and
singing lessons with
the guitar.

Mrs. Plum read stories to them,
gave them some easy math,
and shared her chocolates.
When the box was empty,
she opened her suitcase
and took out another.

21

By the end of the day

the children could not believe their luck.

Mrs. Plum was the best teacher they had ever had.

The best in the school,

in the town,

in the universe!

Yes, everything was perfect.

Well, *almost* everything.

The only trouble was

that in all the excitement

a few little things . . .

had disappeared.

Billy Turpin had lost his football shoes.

Tracey Appledrop had lost her pencil case.

Gloria Gaskitt had lost her lucky charm bracelet.

But even then, Mrs. Plum

was *so* kind,

    so helpful,

    so sympathetic.

She looked everywhere

in that classroom,

searched high and low,

but with no luck at all.

When home-time came,

the missing things were still missing.

Chapter Four
Mrs. Gaskitt's Luck Continues

Two days later, Mrs. Gaskitt got up again.

Of course, she got up on the day in between as well, but nothing happened then.

Yes . . .

Mrs. Gaskitt got up,

Good morning, Mrs. Gaskitt!

fed the children,

fed the cats,

Thanks, Mrs. Gaskitt!

read the paper,

drank the tea,

heard a familiar sound

out in the street

—*Clink, clink!*—

opened the door,

picked up the milk . . .

. . . and kissed the milkman!

But what about *Mr.* Gaskitt?

Never mind—

he *was* the milkman.

It was his very latest job.

Meanwhile—Oh no!—poor Mrs. Fritter

was falling over in the doctor's waiting room.

The doctor had just said

she was well enough to return to work.

Now Mrs. Fritter had more cuts and bruises

and needed to go back to bed again.

Meanwhile, Mrs. Plum was fit and well.

She played soccer with the boys,

and basketball with the girls.

Shoot, dearie!

At playtime, Mrs. Plum
drank tea in the staff room
with the other teachers.

The other teachers liked Mrs. Plum.
She told them funny stories
about her long life as a teacher,
shared her chocolates,
and helped them to look for things . . .

. . . when they
disappeared.

27

Back at the Gaskitts' house,

the phone was ringing.

Mrs. Gaskitt was outside washing her taxi.

In she ran and picked up the receiver.

Congratulations!

"Congratulations, Mrs. Gaskitt!"

said a man on the phone.

"You have won first prize in our—"

"Wow!" cried Mrs. Gaskitt.

"*Another* lucky day."

Chapter Five
One Little Coupon

Two hours later, a truck

"BEEP, BEEP, I AM REVERSING!"

stopped outside the Gaskitts' house.

It had Mrs. Gaskitt's prize in it:

A COMPLETE HOUSEFUL

OF FURNITURE!

"All I did was fill in one

little coupon," said Mrs. Gaskitt.

"Well, I never," said the driver.

"And put some checks in boxes."

"BEEP, BEEP, I AM AMAZED!"

29

Mrs. Gaskitt's prize filled every room in the house

(and the kitchen twice over).

Horace and his friend went around sitting on things.

They were amazed too.

"She's very lucky, my Mrs.," said Horace.

"I wonder why."

"Perhaps she has a lucky horseshoe,"

said his friend. "Or a rabbit's foot—

or a four-leaf clover."

"Or a ten-leaf clover," said Horace.

"There's no such thing," said his friend.

"Yes, there is."

"No, there isn't."

"Yes, there is."

Meanwhile, back at the school,

it was almost home-time.

Some of the children had their coats on,

some were lined up by the door,

and some . . .

Where's my
skipping rope?

Where's my
lunch box?

. . . were looking for things.

Gus and Gloria were giving Randolph, the class rat,

some clean water and a slice of carrot.

"Now then, dearies," said Mrs. Plum.

"Before you go—a message.

 I'm planning a little trip soon—"

"Hooray!"

"Great, Miss!"

"I love a trip!"

"Where to, Miss?"

"Where we going?"

"Er . . . somewhere nice," said Mrs. Plum.

"A sort of mystery tour."

"Brilliant!"

"A mystery tour!"

"I love a mystery tour!"

"I've been on one before!"

"I've been on two!"

"Bring $20," Mrs. Plum said.

"Tomorrow, if you can."

"I can bring $20, Miss!"

"I can bring fifty!"

"A hundred!"

As the children hurried off,

Mrs. Plum called after them.

"One last thing—make it *cash*, dearies."

She popped a chocolate

into Billy Turpin's mouth.

"No checks."

Chapter Six
Two Thousand Dollars!

The next day Mrs. Gaskitt won:

a vacation for four,

a camper,

a free hairdo,

and a packet of Protts!!

She told her family

and her friends

and her cat all about it.

"All I did was . . ."

Horace was pleased, of course,

and proud of Mrs. Gaskitt.

But he was puzzled too.

"A vacation for *four*—what use is that?

Should be a vacation for five."

"Or six," said his friend.

"Or eleven," said his other friends

outside the window.

Meanwhile, Mrs. Plum had collected

twenty-seven $20 bills from

the children and put them

in a safe place.

On wheels.

The children were excited about the trip,

and excited also about the school fair,

only a day away.

Mr. Blagg, the headmaster,

made a little speech about it

to the whole school.

There would be book stalls and cake stalls,

raffles and ring-the-prize,

a coconut toss, and a costume contest.

There'd be a pet show (with prizes),

maypole dancing,

football for the dads,

and an egg-and-spoon race for the moms.

"Last year, children—Sh!" said Mr. Blagg,

"— we raised $1,943.78 for the school fund."

"Hooray!" the children yelled.

"Sh!" said Mr. Blagg.

"So this time, let's break the record.

Let's make it—Sh!

—two thousand dollars!"

"Hooray!
Hooray!"
the children
yelled again.

39

Just then, up jumped Mrs. Plum.

She couldn't stop herself.

"Two thousand dollars!" she cried,

and her big smile

filled the hall.

"I'll help!"

Chapter Seven
Some Funny Business

At lunchtime, Mrs. Gaskitt
ate her free packet of Protts
and had her free hairdo.
Lucky Mrs. Gaskitt.

Meanwhile—Oh no!—

*un*lucky Mrs. Fritter.

Mrs. Fritter had just popped

into the drugstore for some

painkillers and a bandage.

On her way home and outside the *travel agent's,*

she was knocked flying by a short, wide lady

with charming manners

"Beg pardon, dearie!"

and a huge suitcase.

On wheels.

The lady, however,

was very apologetic and *very* kind.

She helped Mrs. Fritter to her feet

and gave her a chocolate.

Later that afternoon,

Gus and Billy Turpin were in the classroom,

giving Randolph some exercise.

Gloria and Tracey Appledrop were painting a sign

for the Guess the Weight of the Cake competition.

Just then a phone rang.

"A phone, Miss! A phone!"

"Who's calling us?"

"Where is it?"

Well, would you believe it? The phone was ringing

from *inside* Mrs. Plum's suitcase.

"It's playing a tune, Miss!"

"So it is, dearie," said Mrs. Plum,

and she gave the suitcase a kick.

"I know that tune, Miss!"

"Me too!"

"It's the same as Mr. Blagg's phone!"

"Yeah!"

"Only he's *lost* his!"

"So he has, dearie," said Mrs. Plum

and she gave the case another kick.

"I helped him look for it."

Meanwhile, Gus and Gloria and some of the
other children were exchanging glances.
There was some funny business here.
Why did Mrs. Plum not open the case?
Come to think of it, why did she *never* open it
(except on that first morning)?

All of a sudden,

the whole class became suspicious.

They smelled a rat, all right . . .

and it was *not* Randolph.

Chapter Eight
Handsome Horace

The next day,

which was a Saturday,

Mrs. Gaskitt leaped out of bed,

raced downstairs,

flew into the

crowded kitchen:

2 tables,

8 chairs,

25 cartons of Crunchy Mice,

Good morning, Mrs. . . .

fed the children,

fed Horace,

Thanks, Mrs. . . .

read the paper,

read the mail,

opened the back door,

kissed the milkman . . .

Thanks, Mrs. . . . .

. . . and went red in the face.

It was the *wrong* milkman.

Meanwhile, Gus and Gloria

were grooming Horace.

They brushed his coat till it shone,

tied a new pink ribbon around his neck,

and told him how handsome he was.

Horace purred with pride.

He wished his friend

was there to see him.

Later that morning,
Mrs. Gaskitt was
still rushing around—
finding her sneakers,
boiling her egg—
while Gus and Gloria
followed her around and
tried to get her attention.

"It's that substitute teacher, Mom."

"Hm." Mrs. Gaskitt was cooling her egg.

"The one with the suitcase."

"Yes." Mrs. Gaskitt was
putting her sneakers on.

"Which she *never* opens!"

"Ah." Mrs. Gaskitt was

getting a spoon from

the cutlery drawer.

"Well, *we* think . . ."

Mrs. Gaskitt was out

through the door,

". . . she's definitely . . ."

into the garden,

and off down the path

with her egg and spoon.

". . . up to something!"

Chapter Nine
Mrs. Plum Lends a Hand

It was a warm May afternoon.

The school fair was in full swing.

The grand total is now $100!

The maypole dancers were dancing

and delicious smells—

ice cream,

cotton candy,

hot dogs—

filled the air.

The grand total is now $200!

Moms and dads were working hard.
The little kids were rushing
around in
their fancy
costumes.

Grand total $250!

Horace, with his beautiful ribbon,
was lined up with the other pets
in the pet show.
And the money . . . $300!

. . . was
pouring
in.

Meanwhile, Mrs. Gaskitt was winning things.

She guessed the weight of the cake,

"All I did was . . ."

and the number of sweets in a jar.

She won a teddy bear,

a bottle of wine,

three goldfish,

five pounds of grass seed,

and a lawn mower.

1st
PRIZE

$500! -- -- -- --

And Horace saw . . . most of it.

He purred with pride.

"I know her," he told a guinea pig.

"Oh yes." The guinea pig was not
interested in Mrs. Gaskitt.

He had other worries.

"Do I look stupid in this bow?"

"No," said Horace. "Not really."

The guinea pig scowled. "Hm. Bet I do."

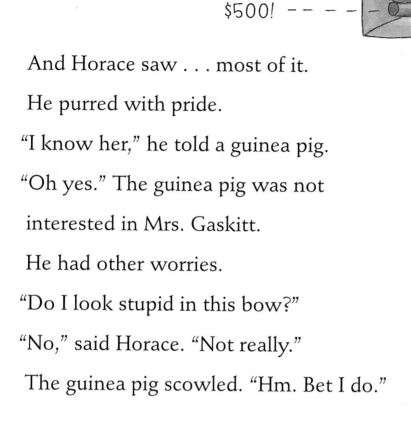

MORRIS.   HORACE.   RON.

But, of course, what (you will be wanting to know),

what about Mrs. Plum?

Well, Mrs. Plum was here,

there, and everywhere.

She helped with

the refreshments.

Where's . . . ?

She helped with

the costumes.

Where's my . . . ?

She helped with

the coconut toss.

The children—Gus and Gloria,

Tracey, Billy, and the others—followed

Mrs. Plum and watched her like hawks.

But the crowds were so big, the noise so loud,

the delicious smells so . . . delicious,

that the children didn't *always* see

what she was up to.

Meanwhile, Mr. Blagg . . .

$1,200!

was looking happier,

$1,300!

and happier,

$1,500!

and happier.

$1,750!

Horace's new friend was looking happier too.

He had just won a rosette.

"So what's your name then?" he asked.

"Horace," said Horace.

"Fancy that—mine's Morris. Horace and Morris!"

"Yeah," said Horace, "all we need is a Boris."

"Or a Doris," said Morris.

"Or a . . . Poris," said Horace.

"*Poris?* There's no such name."

"Yes, there is," said Horace.

"No, there isn't."

Yes, there is.

Now, Mrs. Gaskitt

and the other mothers were lining up . . .

$1,900!

$1,999.99!

. . . for the egg-and-spoon race.

Mr. Blagg

jumped on his chair.

"We've made it—

Sh!" he yelled.

"Grand total—

two thousand

dollars!"

"Hooray! Hooray!"

The crowd cheered, then cheered again

as the egg-and-spoon race began.

It was a tremendous contest.

First Mrs. Turpin was in the lead.

Then she dropped her egg.

Then Mrs. Appledrop was in the lead

and she dropped her egg.

Then Mrs. Gaskitt

was in the lead and . . .

Meanwhile, all eyes (except two)

were on the race.

The children were watching (and yelling).

Horace was watching (and purring with pride).

Even Mr. Blagg on his chair

was watching.

All of a sudden, Mr. Blagg

looked down at the table and

was *not* happy anymore.

The cash box,

the two thousand dollars,

even Mr. Blagg's favorite pencil

(which his dear old mother

had given him) . . .

had disappeared.

Oh no—
Grand total—
$zero!

65

Chapter Ten
Oops!

Now, of course, there was uproar at the school fair.
Everyone was yelling and rushing around.
Well, nearly everyone.

Meanwhile, the egg-and-spoon race
was still in progress.
Mrs. Gaskitt
got up speed,
while her egg,
luckily, stayed on its spoon.
She ran like the wind,
broke the tape, won the race, and—

Oh no!—*collided* with a short, wide lady,

silvery hair,

big smile,

suitcase (on wheels),

and knocked her flying.

Knocked her

suitcase flying too,

which rolled

and bounced

and rolled again . . .

and burst open.

The crowd was astonished . . .

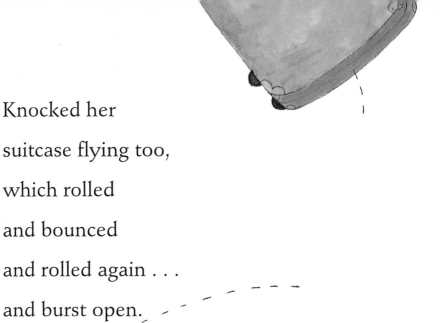

And all that Mrs. Plum,
as she sat on the grass
with an egg in her lap,
could think to say was . . .

Later, when the police arrived, Mrs. Plum had a little more to say.

"Can't think what came over me, dearies."

She smiled at Mr. Blagg.

"Never done anything like this before."

"Yes, you have," said the inspector. "Loads of times."

"She's a very clever woman," the inspector explained.

"Thank you, dearie!"

"Robbed more schools than I've had hot dinners. Been on her trail for ages."

The inspector shook hands with Mr. Blagg and congratulated Mrs. Gaskitt on her lucky collision. "This should put a stop to Mrs. Plum (alias Mrs. Peach, alias Mrs. Pomegranate) and her little games for a while, I shouldn't wonder." He climbed into his police car.

Hm. Where's my whistle?

Chapter Eleven
Mrs. Gaskitt's Luck Runs Out

It was a warm May evening.

Mrs. Gaskitt walked home

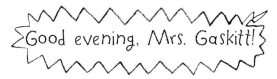

Good evening, Mrs. Gaskitt!

with her children,

her cat, and her prizes.

Gus and Gloria were telling

their mom all about Mrs. Plum.

I can't wait to tell my friend!

1st PRIZE

Mrs. Gaskitt was telling

Gus and Gloria

(and Horace)

how she had won

the teddy bear,

the bottle of wine,

and all the other things.

"All I did . . ."

Suddenly, not looking

where she was going,

Mrs. Gaskitt walked straight under

a window washer's ladder.

Oh no!—*un*lucky Mrs. Gaskitt.

Water from the window
washer's bucket
came splashing down
and soaked her to the skin.

And that wasn't the end of it.
Next thing, would you believe it,
the *window washer himself*
came scrambling down,
grabbed Mrs. Gaskitt,
hauled her to her feet—
and kissed her!

But what about *Mr.* Gaskitt?
Well, you've guessed it,
haven't you?
Yes—it was
his latest job.

Meanwhile, Horace was thinking hard . . .

about luck.

"Hm. Lucky rabbit's foot—no.

Lucky horseshoes—no.

Lucky four-leaf clovers—no.

Lucky black cats . . ."

It was a warm May night.

The Gaskitts were asleep

in their crowded bedrooms.

The goldfish were getting

used to their new home.

The garage was full of grass seed.

Horace and his friend were

downstairs playing cards.

Slapjack!

"It's you!" said Horace.

"What is?" said his friend. "Slapjack!—I win."

"That's it—you always win!" said Horace.

"You're the *lucky black cat*!"

"No, I'm not—Slapjack!" said his friend.

"Yes, you are."

"No, I'm not."

"Yes, you are."

"No, I'm not."

"Yes, you are."

"No, I'm . . . not!"

"Yes . . . you . . . *yawn* . . . are."

LEVEL 3
J

Ahlberg, Allan

The Woman Who Won Things

$14.99